RUNS FROM GUNS

STORY BY
Emily Fischer

PAINTINGS BY
Lisa Madenspacher

ISBN# 1-930710-29-1
Copyright ©2000 Veritas Press

Veritas Press
1250 Belle Meade Drive
Lancaster, PA 17601

First edition

RUNS
☞ FROM
GUNS

STORY BY
Emily Fischer

PAINTINGS BY
Lisa Madenspacher

Veritas Press

This book is dedicated to my
husband who told me this
story and many others.

"A cannon ball has hit my wall.
A cannon shell is in my well.
Cannon shot is on my lot!"
Sad Will sits in shock.

Up in the attic Will can watch the combat.
The Rebs run back from the Feds.
They run and run from the attack.

The Feds will catch them. The Feds will win if the Rebs fall back.

Then Will watches as Jackson will not run. Jackson will not fall back. He is as a rock wall. Then the Rebs will not run.

Then and there the Rebs attack with
"Rockwall" Jackson.
The Feds have met a match!
Will watches men rush on his lot.

There is a lot he
wishes he had hid!
Will rushes to put
up this and that.
He shuts his
chicks in his shed.

Will tucks his watch
in the shucks.

He puts his cash
in his radish patch.

Then the Rebs dash in his cabin.
Lots of men rush in. Will lets the
Rebs use his cabin. A thin chap washes
a gash in his leg in Will's bath tub.

Maps are on his bed.
Men fill his shop with
guns and shells.

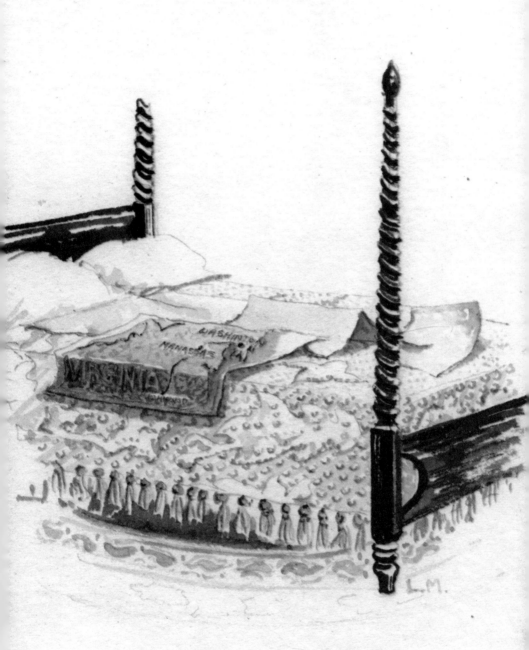

18

Men use his kitchen.
One whips up a
dish of fish and
a pot of mush.

19

On a bench Jackson has
a chat with Jon E. Reb.
"Rockwall Jackson is in my cabin!"
yells Will. Then the shells let up.

The guns hush. As quick as they ran on, the Rebs run off Will's lot. The Feds have given up and fallen back. Yet the Feds will be back. The guns and cannons will be back. Will loves his cabin but not the havoc of the combat. He wishes to go from guns and shells and cannons.

Will packs his wagon with his jugs, pots,
and pans. He puts his bed and bath tub in
the wagon. The rig is full of rugs and mats.

Will hitches an ox to the wagon. The ox pulls him from the combat. The ox pulls him to a lot at Appomattox. There Will can set up a cabin that will not be by the Feds and the Rebs. There cannons will not bash his wall, and he will not get shot.

Will gets a mutt to watch his lot.
His mutt has six pups. The pups have pups.
There are lots and lots of mutts
to watch Will's cabin.

Then...

Gun men go up Will's path to his
cabin. The mutts yip and yap.
"Not the Feds and the Rebs! I have to be
from the combat that was at
my cabin in Manassas."
The men tell Will they
have to use his cabin.
They tell Will that
the Feds and Rebs
will not attack there.

The men will pen a bill to finish the
combat. In Will's den the top men chat.
The Rebs put in pen that they will quit
the combat. The Feds have won.

The Rebs call off man by man and give the Feds their guns. The top men tell the Rebs to go back to their cabins. Will is sad that Rockwall Jackson is not there. Rockwall Jackson was shot in the combat.

Lots of Feds and Rebs did perish in the combat. Lots of men will not go back to the ones that love them. Yet all is not sadness. The combat has let up. The gun shots and cannon shells will not be back.

The Feds and the Rebs can patch up the ill will. As the men go off Will shuts the latch to his cabin. Will mulls on the Feds and the Rebs and the combat. Will sat in his cabin to watch the kick-off of the combat at Manassas. Thus the combat finishes in his den at Appomattox.